Which potty is Ian's?

Which underpants are Ian's?

To: Ian, congratulations!

First published in Belgium and Holland by Clavis Uitgeverij, Hasselt – Amsterdam, 2010
Copyright © 2010, Clavis Uitgeverij

English translation from the Dutch by Clavis Publishing Inc. New York
Copyright © 2011 for the English language edition: Clavis Publishing Inc. New York

Visit us on the web at www.clavisbooks.com – www.paulineoud.nl

Ian's New Potty written and illustrated by Pauline Oud
Original title: *Kas op het potje*
Translated from the Dutch by Clavis Publishing
English language edition edited by Emma D. Dryden, drydenbks llc

ISBN 978-1-60537-103-0
This book was printed in August 2012 at Proost, Everdongenlaan 23, B-2300 Turnhout, Belgium

First Edition
10 9 8 7 6 5 4 3 2

Ian's
New Potty

Pauline Oud

Clavis

NEW YORK

"Look at this, Ian," Mommy says, "I bought you big boys' underpants. And do you know what this is?"

Ian sees a big, red potty.

"Ha!" Ian says. "I know! It's a potty. I can sit on it and then pee will come."

Ian takes the potty and underwear into the bathroom.
"Look, Flap," Ian says to his rabbit, "this potty is mine."
Ian puts the potty on the floor and sits down on it.
"If you sit on the potty, you have to pee."

Ian and Flap wait for Ian's pee to come.
They wait ...
    and wait ...
        and wait.

"Mommy!" Ian calls. "The pee is not coming!"

"Oh, that's alright," Mommy says. "It doesn't always happen right away. Put on your underpants and go have some fun. You can try again later to pee in the potty."

Ian starts to build a tower with his blocks. "Look at this, Flap. My tower is really, really high. I'm going to make it even higher so it's a big boys' tower."

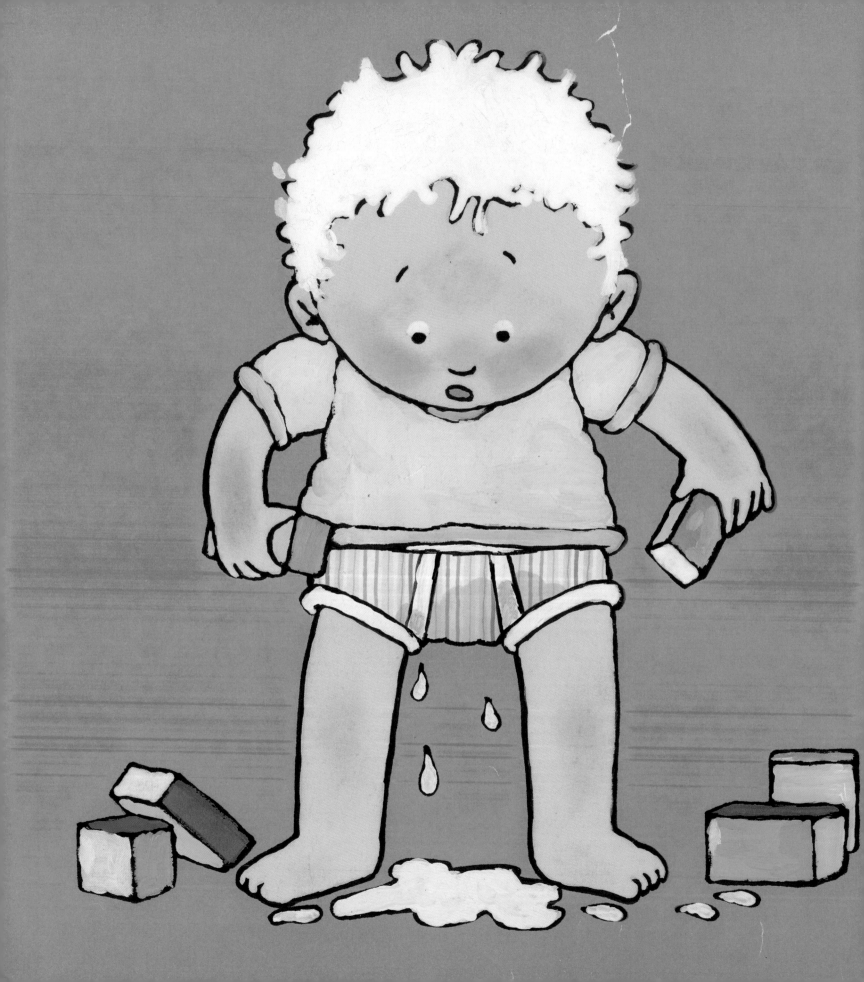

Ian adds more blocks.
The tower is getting taller and taller.
But—what's that funny feeling?
Something tickles in Ian's belly.
All of a sudden, Ian's underpants are wet.
So is the floor.
"Uh-oh," Ian says. "I think I had to pee."

Mommy gives Ian another pair of underpants.
Ian's baby sister gets a new diaper. She is still very little.
Just like Flap.
"Look at this, Flap," Ian says. "These underpants
have cars on them. Zoom! Zoom! These are
big boys' underpants!"

Ian, Mommy, and the baby are having lunch.
The baby is drinking a bottle of milk and Ian is
drinking juice from his green cup.
Mom has made him a delicious sandwich.

"Look, Flap," Ian says. "What a big sandwich this is! This is a sandwich for big boys."

Ian takes a big bite. He has a big boys' appetite.

After lunch, Mommy gives Ian a piece of rope, some clothespins, and an old sheet.

"Look at this," Ian says to Flap. "I'm building a tent. This is a big boys' tent."

But—what's that funny feeling? Something tickles in Ian's belly.

"Uh-oh," Ian says. "I have to pee!"
Quickly Ian runs to the bathroom.
"Look, Flap, there's my potty!"

Ian pulls down his underpants and sits on his potty.
Pssshhh!
What is that Ian and Flap hear?
"That is pee!" Ian says.
Plop!
Is that more pee?

Ian stands up and looks into his potty.
"Look at that, Flap! I did more than
pee! Mommy! Mommy!" Ian yells.
"Come quick! See what I did!"

"Good for you, Ian!" Mommy says happily. "You did pee and poop. You did very well!"

Mommy wipes Ian's bottom all clean with toilet paper.

"You can pull your underpants up now," Mommy says.

Ian's big boys' underpants are still clean and dry.

Mommy takes the potty and empties it in the toilet.

"Just climb on the stool, Ian," Mommy says, "and you can flush the toilet."

Ian pushes the button and flushes the toilet.

Whoosh!

The toilet water washes Ian's pee and poop away.

"Bye-bye!" Ian says.

Ian is not finished yet.
He still has to wash his hands.
Ian moves the stool so he can
reach the sink. Mmmm, the
soap smells so sweet!

Ian turns off the light and closes the door behind him.
"Look, Flap! I'm a big boy now! And I'm ready to play!"